The Mummy Walks

Look for more books in the Goosebumps Series 2000
by R.L. Stine:

#1 *Cry of the Cat*
#2 *Bride of the Living Dummy*
#3 *Creature Teacher*
#4 *Invasion of the Body Squeezers, Part I*
#5 *Invasion of the Body Squeezers, Part II*
#6 *I Am Your Evil Twin*
#7 *Revenge R Us*
#8 *Fright Camp*
#9 *Are You Terrified Yet?*
#10 *Headless Halloween*
#11 *Attack of the Graveyard Ghouls*
#12 *Brain Juice*
#13 *Return to HorrorLand*
#14 *Jekyll and Heidi*
#15 *Scream School*

The Mummy Walks

AN
APPLE
PAPERBACK

SCHOLASTIC INC.
New York Toronto London Auckland
Sydney New Delhi Hong Kong

A PARACHUTE PRESS BOOK

No part of this publication may be reproduced in whole or in part, or stored in a retrieval system, or transmitted in any form or by any means, electronic, mechanical, photocopying, recording, or otherwise, without written permission of the publisher. For information regarding permission, write to Scholastic Inc., Attention: Permissions Department, 557 Broadway, New York, NY 10012.

ISBN-13: 978-0-590-68520-7

Copyright © 1999 by Parachute Press, Inc.
APPLE PAPERBACKS and Logo are trademarks and/or registered trademarks of Scholastic Inc.
GOOSEBUMPS is a registered trademark of Parachute Press, Inc.

This edition is for sale in Indian subcontinent only.

First Scholastic printing, April 1999
Reprinted by Scholastic India Pvt. Ltd., September 2007
March 2008; January; August 2010; May 2011; January 2012
July; December 2013; September; December 2014; July
December 2015

Printed at JJ Offset Printers, Noida

"You'll be fine, Michael," Mom said.

It was the *hundredth* time she said it!

We walked past the lines of people in front of the ticket counters. Everyone in the airport seemed to be in a desperate hurry.

I watched a young couple run toward the gates. Their suitcases bounced on tiny wheels behind them.

A man and woman stood near the security station, pawing through their carry-on bags, arguing loudly.

"I thought *you* had the tickets. I gave them to you this morning!"

"No. You idiot — I told *you* to bring them!"

As Mom, Dad, and I hurried past, I saw a little girl sitting on top of a stack of suitcases, crying.

Her parents were pleading with her, begging her to stop.

Dad carried my canvas duffel bag. He turned to talk to me — and stumbled over a luggage cart.

I laughed.

Dad looked so funny.

Why did everyone have to be so tense?

Dad dropped my duffel bag onto the conveyor belt. We walked through the security gate. Dad set off the buzzer.

Rolling his eyes, he took his keys from his pocket and tried again. This time he made it through.

I watched my bag on the TV screen. When it went through the X ray, I could see everything in the bag. It was totally cool!

He picked up my bag, and we walked down the long hall to the gate. Mom and Dad were walking so fast, I had to jog to keep up.

"Aunt Sandra will be there to meet you in Orlando," Mom said. "You'll see her as soon as you get off the plane."

"I know, I know," I groaned.

How many times had we gone over this plan? At least a thousand!

I'd spent the last two weeks thinking about all the things I wanted to do in Orlando. Of course, Disney World was at the top of the list. But I wanted to spend a lot of time at Sea World too.

I'm really into fish and life under the sea. When

Mom and Dad took me snorkeling in the Bahamas last summer, I totally freaked. I mean, there's this whole beautiful world down there with all these amazing creatures! It was like traveling to another planet.

Dad says I'd make a good astronaut. He says I'm a real explorer. And he's right. I love going to new places, discovering new things.

So why are they making such a big deal about me flying to Orlando by myself?

We reached the gate. Dad set down the bag. He glanced nervously at his watch.

Mom squeezed my arm. "Don't worry," she said.

"I'm *not* worrying!" I insisted. "What is your problem? I'm twelve years old, you know!"

Mom and Dad exchanged glances. Mom bit her bottom lip. She had already chewed all her lipstick off.

"*Last boarding call for Flight 501 to Pittsburgh,*" a woman's voice blared on the loudspeaker. "*Flight 501 is boarding through Gate 45.*"

"You've never flown by yourself before," Dad said. "We've always been with you."

"I'm not worried," I assured them again. "It's not too hard. I just sit in my seat, and in a couple of hours I'll be in Orlando."

I laughed. "The pilots have to do all the work. Not me."

Mom and Dad didn't laugh. "You're sitting in First Class," Mom said. "So you'll be comfortable."

"That's cool," I replied. "This guy at school told me they serve ice cream sundaes in First Class."

"Maybe," Dad said, glancing at his watch again. He raised his eyes to the gate. "Time for you to board."

Mom let out a little cry and wrapped her arms around me. "Have a good, safe trip, Michael," she whispered, pressing her cheek against mine. When she pulled back, I saw that she had tears in her eyes.

Dad hugged me too. He cleared his throat, but he didn't say anything.

"I'll be fine," I told them again. "I'll call you from Aunt Sandra's."

Mom handed me a white envelope. Dad picked up my duffel bag and walked me up to the gate. "You're in seat 1-A," he told me. He gave me the duffel bag and patted me on the shoulder.

I turned and waved to them. Mom was wiping tears off her cheeks with both hands.

"I'll be fine. Really!" I called to her. Then I turned and headed down the boarding tunnel to the plane.

Wow, I thought. Why are they so *weird*? Am I the first kid in history to fly to Orlando by himself?

I didn't see any flight attendants as I stepped into the plane. But my seat was easy to find. It was the very first seat in the front row of the First Class section.

I jammed my duffel bag into the overhead compartment. Then I dropped into the seat.

Wow. Comfortable.

I'm going to enjoy this, I decided.

I leaned into the aisle, searching for a flight attendant. I wanted to ask if they were going to show a movie.

No one there yet.

I fiddled with the seatbelt, trying to loosen it. Finally, I got it right and clicked it into place. I settled back against the soft leather seat.

And remembered the envelope my mom had given me. I had jammed it into my jeans pocket.

I pulled it out and studied it. A plain white envelope.

Was it a letter? Did Mom and Dad write me a note or something?

I tore the envelope open and pulled out a sheet of paper.

I unfolded it, brought it close to my face — and my heart skipped a beat as I gazed in shock at the short message:

WE ARE NOT YOUR PARENTS.

"H uh?"

I gripped the paper between my two hands and stared at the words until they blurred.

"This is a joke — right?" I murmured to myself.

Mom and Dad were always teasing me because I don't look like them. They're both tall and blond. And I have dark-brown hair and brown eyes, and I'm kind of short and kind of chubby.

But this was a very strange joke.

I read the short note again. Then I read it out loud: "We are not your parents."

It was written in blue ink in a large, looping script. My dad's handwriting.

I realized that my hands were suddenly trembling.

I folded up the note and shoved it into my pocket.

"Weird," I muttered. "Weird."

Why would Mom and Dad write that? What does it mean?

"We are not your parents."

If it was a joke, I didn't get it.

I'll ask Aunt Sandra about it, I decided. Or maybe I'll call Mom and Dad as soon as I get to Orlando and ask them what it meant.

"We are not your parents."

My stomach felt a little queasy. My heart fluttered.

I leaned into the aisle again. Still no flight attendants.

I raised myself in the seat and glanced around the cabin.

No one else in First Class. I counted four rows of empty gray seats.

Am I the only one flying First Class? I wondered.

Orlando is a popular place. Where is everyone?

My throat suddenly felt dry. I wanted a glass of water. But there was no one to ask.

I unclasped the seatbelt, let the belt drop to the cushion, and stood up. The floor vibrated beneath me. I could hear the engine warming up.

A heavy red curtain separated First Class from Coach. I made my way to the curtain and pushed it aside.

I poked my head into the Coach cabin. Shafts of sunlight poured through the double rows of windows.

Empty. No one there.

No one.

"Hey —" I called out, squeezing the curtain in my hand. "Hey — anyone here?"

My voice sounded tiny in the big, empty cabin. The rumble and whine of the jet engine was the only other sound.

"Hey —"

I let the curtain drop back into place and turned back to the front. "Anybody here?" I called. "What's going on?"

Silence.

No sign of anyone.

There's some mistake, I decided. I'm on the wrong plane or something.

I've got to get off this plane.

I reached up and started to tug my duffel bag from the overhead bin.

I was still tugging when I heard a loud, scraping sound — then a *WHOOSH* of air.

I gasped as the airplane door slammed shut.

"Wait! Let me out of here!" I cried. "Let me out!"

dropped my bag and lurched to the door.

"Let me out!" I cried again, shouting over the roar of the engine. "Hey — somebody!"

I pounded on the door.

And fell back against the bathroom as the plane began to move.

We're backing up, I realized. Backing away from the gate.

"No, wait!" I screamed.

I spun toward the cockpit door.

I have to tell the pilot that no one else is on-board, I decided.

I have to make him stop the plane!

It's a mistake. A big mistake!

I knocked on the door, softly at first. Then harder.

9

"Hey —" I called in. "You've got to stop! There's no one here! Hey — can you hear me?"

No reply.

I pressed a hand against the wall to steady myself as the plane turned, backing up.

"Can you hear me?" I shrieked. "I'm all alone back here!"

My dry throat ached from screaming. I swallowed hard. Took a deep breath. And then pounded with both fists on the cockpit door.

"Listen to me! Stop the plane! Stop it!"

No reply. Not a sound.

Someone has to be in there, I knew.

Someone is piloting this plane.

I grabbed the cockpit door handle. Frantically tried to pull it open.

The door wouldn't budge.

I leaned my shoulder against it. Tried to push it open.

No.

Was it locked?

Why would the pilots lock themselves inside?

My heart thudded in my chest. I swallowed again, my throat as dry and scratchy as steel wool.

"Please!" I called in to the cockpit. "Why won't you listen to me?"

The plane lurched and I tumbled against the bathroom door again.

As I pulled myself up, I heard a loudspeaker crackle to life.

10

"Please take your seat for takeoff."

A man's voice.

"No! You don't understand!" I wailed. I pounded again on the cockpit door. "There's been a mistake!"

Loud static made me cover my ears. Then through the static, the man's voice repeated his order: "Please take your seat. We cannot take off until you are in your seat."

I hesitated.

They aren't going to listen to me, I realized.

They aren't going to talk to me.

With a weary sigh, I slumped into my seat. I was still buckling the seatbelt when I felt the plane take off.

"I don't believe this," I muttered.

I turned to the window and saw the ground slant away.

Up, up. The blue sky filled the round window.

I peered down at the airport, the surrounding trees, the square blocks of houses, tiny like dollhouses now.

This isn't happening, I told myself.

I'm all alone. All alone on this huge jet plane.

I could feel the air pressure change as the plane began to climb.

It turned sharply. I heard the engines whine louder.

The plane tilted slowly. Dipped to one side. Then straightened out. Turning . . . turning . . .

Peering down, I saw that the square blocks of houses had vanished.

I saw green treetops. Empty fields. Then more treetops.

Then a long, narrow strip of yellow.

Beach? Yes. The long, sandy beach along the Atlantic.

I stared down, frozen in place.

We were heading out over the ocean now. Sunlight sparkled, casting sheets of gold over the rolling blue-green waters, making the whole ocean shimmer and gleam.

Why are we flying over the ocean? I wondered.

And then I realized: We're not flying to Orlando.

This can't be the way to Orlando.

I slumped down in the seat, my hands clammy and wet, clasped tightly together in my lap. I took a long, deep breath and held it, trying to slow down my racing heart.

Where are we going?

Where?

And then, as I took another deep breath, I saw the pilot's door slowly open. . . .

man stepped out from the cockpit. His dark eyes narrowed, examining me coldly.

He looked about forty, older than my dad. He had straight, shiny black hair streaked with white, pulled back in a long ponytail. His black mustache came down around the sides of his mouth and was also streaked with white.

He was very tanned. A tiny diamond stud sparkled in one earlobe.

He wore a green-and-black camouflage jacket over baggy khakis. He had two rows of silver medals pinned to the right breast of his jacket.

"Wh-who are you?" I managed to choke out.

He continued to study me with those jet-black eyes. He didn't reply.

"What's going on?" I demanded. "Where is everybody? Where is this plane going?"

He raised both hands and motioned for me to relax. "All in good time," he said. He had a surprisingly soft voice with a hint of a foreign accent.

"But — I don't understand!" I sputtered.

Again, he motioned for me to relax. His hands were as tanned as his face.

He turned to the small galley and pulled a plastic tray from a shelf. "It is a long flight. I will prepare a lunch for you."

I jumped to my feet, my heart pounding. My knees suddenly felt weak, as if they were about to collapse.

"I don't want lunch!" I screamed in a high, shrill voice. "I want out of here! Turn this plane around! There's been a terrible mistake!"

He raised a finger to his lips. "Shhh." He opened a refrigerator and pulled out a sandwich wrapped in foil. "What would you like to drink?"

"I don't want a drink!" I shrieked. "I want to get off this plane! I want to go home! This is a mistake!"

"It is no mistake," he said softly. He placed a can of Coke on the tray.

"It *has* to be a mistake!" I insisted. "I'm supposed to meet my aunt in Orlando! Who are you? What is this flight? Where are we going?"

He set down the tray and turned to me. "My

name is Lieutenant Henry," he replied, bowing his head slightly. "I am sorry. That is all I am allowed to tell you, Excellency."

"Huh? Excellency?" I frowned at him. "Why did you call me that?"

He didn't answer.

He's crazy! I decided.

He's some kind of lunatic. He and a pilot have hijacked this plane. I'm being kidnapped or something!

My knees gave way. I dropped back into the seat. I took a deep breath, trying to slow my racing heart.

"Do not be frightened," Lieutenant Henry said. "You will be told all, Excellency. You will learn everything in due time."

Excellency?

What was he *talking* about?

"Here." He set the tray in my lap. "Have some lunch. It's a very long flight."

Lieutenant Henry disappeared back into the cockpit and didn't return.

We flew all night. I tilted the seat back and tried to sleep. But I was too frightened.

What is going on? I asked myself. That weird note from my parents . . . the empty plane . . . this man calling me *Excellency* . . .

I stared out the window. I could see a pale half-moon, trails of gray mist curling over it. Dark ocean below. Endless ocean, gleaming brightly in the moonlight.

I finally fell into a deep, dreamless sleep. When I awoke, red sunlight was streaming through the small, round window.

I peered out. The ocean had been replaced by another kind of sea — a sea of yellow and white sand.

"Desert," I murmured.

The pilot's door opened. I saw the back of a man's head in the pilot's seat. Red hair falling out from under a black baseball cap.

Lieutenant Henry stepped out and closed the door, blocking my view.

"Did you sleep, Excellency?" he asked, nodding his head in another short bow.

The plane bounced. He steadied himself with one hand against the cabin wall. As he raised his arm, I glimpsed a brown leather gun holster under his jacket.

Oh, wow, I thought.

The plane really is being hijacked.

Does he plan to shoot me when we land? Is he going to hold me for ransom?

He's in for a surprise. My parents both work. They don't have much ransom money.

"Did you sleep?" he repeated.

"I guess," I replied, stretching my hands over

my head. "Where are we? What desert is that down there?"

He turned into the galley. "We will be landing soon," he replied. He gave me breakfast — orange juice, an apple, and a bowl of cornflakes with milk. Then he disappeared back into the cockpit.

As I spooned up the cereal, I peered down at the yellow sand. White rocks poked up through the sand like bones. As we slowly dropped, the shadow of the plane slid over the sand, a long gray shadow.

We bounced down on a small runway between two low yellow hills. The plane hit hard. The milk splashed out of my cereal bowl.

I could see a long white stucco airport. As we rolled to a stop, I saw a row of green Jeeps. Brown-uniformed soldiers with rifles. Clusters of people in white robes.

The plane stopped with a jolt. I was thrown forward against the seatbelt.

Lieutenant Henry appeared in the cockpit doorway. "Sorry about the landing, Excellency," he said. "The runway is a bit too short for this large plane."

"Where are we?" I demanded angrily. "Why did you bring me here? Why do you keep calling me Excellency?"

"Come," he said, motioning for me to undo the seatbelt. The cabin door slid open. Bright sunlight streamed in. "I'm sure that General Rameer will explain everything to you."

I unbuckled the belt, but I didn't stand up. "Am I being kidnapped? Am I?"

He smiled for the first time. His dark eyes flashed merrily, as if I had made a joke.

"Of course not," he replied.

Lieutenant Henry led me out into the bright sunlight. As we stepped onto a metal stairway, I had to shield my eyes from the glare. A blast of hot, dry air greeted me.

Our shoes clanged down the stairway. Four stern-looking soldiers met us at the bottom. Lieutenant Henry nodded to them. They gave him a two-fingered salute.

Standing back by the little airport, I saw a crowd of people. Some were in white robes. Some were in camouflage shirts and pants. Some wore brightly colored shirts and shorts.

They all were cheering. Many of them waved green pennant-shaped banners. At the side of the building, a small band was playing.

Was this all for *me*?

"This is totally *crazy*," I murmured.

With Lieutenant Henry at my side, I followed the four soldiers across the airfield. They led us to a long black limousine parked at the end of the runway.

A dark-uniformed driver bowed and pulled

open the back door of the enormous car. The soldiers stepped aside, walking stiffly in rhythm.

"Get in, Excellency," Lieutenant Henry urged. "Climb into the car. General Rameer awaits you."

I hesitated. The hot sun beamed down on me, but I still felt a cold chill run down my back.

I'm a million miles from home, I thought. Nowhere to run. No way to escape.

I lowered my head and peered into the car.

Sitting on the red leather seat was a large, smiling man in a white linen suit. He had curly white hair above a slender, tanned face. A stubble of dark beard on his cheeks and chin. Flashing black eyes.

He held a shiny black cane between his legs. A green-jeweled ring sparkled on the pinky finger of his right hand.

He waved for me to climb in beside him. "Welcome, Excellency," he called out in a hoarse voice.

I leaned into the doorway. "Why are you calling me that?" I cried.

And then I couldn't hold it back. All of my anger, all of my fear and confusion burst out of me.

"I demand to see my parents!" I screamed. "I'm not getting into your car! I want to talk to my parents *right now*!"

General Rameer's smile faded quickly. His eyes dulled. His whole face appeared to darken.

"I'm sorry, Michael," he said softly. "Your parents are no longer alive."

5

I gasped. And grabbed the limo door to steady myself.

"Huh? My parents —?"

General Rameer nodded sadly.

"But — they took me to the airport in New York yesterday!" I cried. "They saw me onto the plane and —"

"Do you mean the Clarkes? Those people are not your parents, Excellency," General Rameer said.

"Not my parents?"

"They were supposed to let you know the truth before you boarded the plane."

The note!

We are not your parents.

Was it *true*?

"But — I — I —" I sputtered, still gripping the limo door for support.

"Get in," General Rameer urged. "I will not harm you. There is no need to be afraid, Michael."

"Climb in," Lieutenant Henry also urged, placing a firm hand on my trembling shoulder.

I gazed back toward the airport. The crowd was still cheering. The green pennants waved. The band continued to play a happy march.

The sun pounded down on me. My head throbbed painfully. I suddenly felt as if I were melting, melting into the tar of the runway.

I took a deep breath and climbed into the red leather seat beside General Rameer.

The limo door closed behind me. I felt a cold burst of air from the air-conditioning.

I turned to General Rameer. His white suit gleamed. He gripped his shiny ebony cane tightly with both hands.

He nodded to the driver. The car began to roll across the runway. Past the band and the crowd of cheering people.

I couldn't see them clearly now. The limo windows were tinted dark gray.

"My parents —" I started.

"Don't worry about the Clarkes," General Rameer said softly. "They will be treated well."

"You mean — they're okay?" I gasped.

The general nodded. "They are being well paid

for protecting you. They did a good job for the past twelve years."

"Uh . . . protecting me?"

"They hid you and they protected you," General Rameer replied.

I squinted out the tinted window, my mind whirring, trying to understand.

The big limo bounced over a narrow road. I saw rows of small white houses on one side of the car. The rolling sands of the desert stretched endlessly out the other window.

I saw people walking along the side of the road. They turned and stared at the limo as we bounced by.

"I — I don't believe any of this," I stammered, shaking my head.

He patted my arm. His eyes watered. His face suddenly revealed real sadness.

"I know this must be hard for you," he said in his hoarse, whispery voice. "I know this must come as a terrible shock."

"So . . . Mom and Dad — I mean, the Clarkes —" I started.

"They took you away to the United States," General Rameer interrupted, his dark eyes locked on mine. "You were a baby. You cannot remember. They escaped with you to New York. They had their orders."

"Orders?"

"To protect you. To keep our enemies from finding you. To bring you up as a normal boy."

"And my real parents?" I asked.

He lowered his head until his forehead touched the tip of his cane. "Your real parents were killed in the war."

I swallowed hard. "War?"

"Our twelve-year struggle with the rebel forces. Our twelve-year battle against those who would take control and destroy our nation."

I stared at him, sweat pouring down my forehead despite the air-conditioning.

Struggling to take this all in. Struggling to make sense of what he was telling me.

"What is this nation?" I asked finally. "What is it called?"

His face brightened. "Jezekiah," he told me. "Jezekiah. It is your homeland, Michael. It is *your* nation."

"I — I'm very confused," I confessed. I clasped my cold, clammy hands together in my lap.

"It is to be expected," General Rameer said, nodding. "But the news is all good, Excellency. You see, after twelve years of war, we have won. It is finally safe for you to return and lead your people."

I swallowed again. Was this all a joke? A lie?

I stared deep into the general's eyes, searching for the truth. But I could see only my own reflection.

"Am I really the leader of this nation?" I finally choked out. "Is it true?"

He nodded. "Yes. We are driving to the Royal Palace. You will take your place as the ruler of Jezekiah."

He gripped my arm tightly. "But first, you must prove that you really are Michael. You must prove that you really are the royal prince."

I uttered a short gasp. "Prove it? How?"

He squeezed my arm. "It is an easy test. You must tell us the location of the mummy."

I gaped at him. "Mummy? *What* mummy?"

The limo pulled through a tall iron gate onto a long, paved driveway. Two rows of palm trees leaned over us as we rolled slowly up to the Royal Palace.

My mouth dropped open as the palace came into view. An endless pink-and-white building of towers and turrets and gated courtyards. All along the drive, brown-uniformed soldiers stood guard at stiff attention, rifles raised at their waists.

As we passed a wide courtyard, I saw a bubbling waterfall splashing into a huge, tear-shaped swimming pool. Tall shrubs and clumps of palm trees provided shade all along the walk that led to the brass double doors at the front.

"This is your home, Excellency," General Rameer said quietly. "I see you are overwhelmed."

"I don't believe any of this," I confessed.

He chuckled, but his expression remained solemn. "I hope it works out for you," he muttered under his breath.

"In ancient times, our people made mummies of the dead, just as the Egyptians did," General Rameer explained.

The two of us were in the dining room, an enormous room with gold-papered walls, silvery curtains, and a crystal chandelier that appeared to float over us. We were seated across from each other at one end of a long, polished mahogany table.

Servants had brought out lunch — bowls piled high with fruit, dates and figs, plates of roast chicken and lamb, salads, potatoes, and rice.

When I sat down, I didn't think I could eat. My stomach felt tied in knots. My head was still swimming from everything that I'd heard and seen.

But I was hungrier than I thought. After all, I hadn't eaten a real meal for nearly a day. I piled my plate high. General Rameer seemed pleased to see me eat so hungrily.

And as I ate, he explained to me about the mummy.

"The mummy of the Emperor Pukrah is a national treasure, Michael," he said, spreading a thick brown paste onto a slice of flatbread. "Pukrah was an ancient leader. Pukrah's mummy is the oldest one known in the world."

General Rameer tore off an end of the bread and handed it to me. The pasty stuff had a strange taste, sweet and spicy at the same time.

"Pukrah's mummy was kept for centuries in this palace," the general continued. "Then, twelve years ago, the rebels began their war. Your parents — our rulers — decided the mummy was no longer safe.

"They knew the rebels were desperate to capture the mummy. So your parents decided to hide the mummy where neither side could find it. And they hid something of priceless value inside the mummy."

I swallowed a slice of chicken. Then I scooped some of the spicy potato salad onto my plate. "What did they hide?" I asked.

General Rameer tore a cluster of grapes from the bowl and popped them one by one into his mouth. "Your parents opened the mummy and hid the Jezekiah Sapphire inside."

"The *what*?" I asked.

"It is the most beautiful jewel in the world," General Rameer gushed, clapping his hands together. He suddenly had a dreamy look in his eyes. "The sapphire is so valuable, our entire treasury is based on it."

I squinted across the table at him. I didn't really know what he meant. But I could see by the expression on his face that the Jezekiah Sapphire had to be worth big bucks.

"Our nation cannot survive without it," General Rameer said, leaning close. "For twelve years, the war was fought. The rebels searched desperately for Pukrah's mummy. They knew if they found the mummy — and the jewel — that victory was theirs.

"But your parents hid the mummy well. It was not found." He sighed and picked up another handful of grapes.

"Now the war is nearly ended," he said in his hoarse voice. "A few rebels remain. But we have won. We must find the mummy and claim the sapphire."

I dropped my fork. "You mean — *you* don't know where it's hidden?"

General Rameer shook his head. "Your parents didn't tell anyone. And then they died as the war began. No one here knows the mummy's hiding place. Not me. Not any of the other generals."

He leaned even closer, and his dark eyes burned into mine. "We must have that mummy. Our nation cannot survive without it."

He grabbed my wrist tightly. "And you, Michael. You are the only one who knows where it is hidden."

"Huh? I do?" I tried to free my arm. But he kept his tight grasp on my wrist, his eyes frozen on mine.

"You were a tiny baby. Your parents planted a

memory chip in your brain telling the mummy's hiding place. Then you were rushed away to the United States where the secret would be safe."

"Oh. I see." What a lame reply.

But what was I supposed to say?

My mouth suddenly felt dry as cotton again. I took a long drink from the crystal water goblet.

General Rameer finally let go of my wrist. But he didn't turn away his gaze. He didn't blink. He stared at me as if trying to find the mummy's hiding place in my eyes.

"It is good to have you back where you belong," he said, forcing a short, tense smile. "What a pity that your parents cannot see what a fine young man you have grown to be."

"Uh . . . thank you," I replied awkwardly. I took another long drink. A servant stepped forward with a silver pitcher to refill my glass.

"Now you will lead us to the mummy and the sapphire," General Rameer said. "And the nation will be so happy to have you — its true leader — back home."

"Uh . . . yeah," I replied, nervously ruffling the white linen napkin in my lap.

"Do you wish to tell me the mummy's hiding place now?" General Rameer asked softly. "All of Jezekiah is waiting to hear."

I took a deep breath. "Well . . ."

I froze in panic. My heart did a flip-flop in my chest.

Do I know where the mummy is? I asked myself.

No. No way. I don't have a clue.

General Rameer stared at me, waiting. Waiting for my answer.

All of Jezekiah is waiting for my answer, I realized, gripping the edge of the table.

When they find out I don't know anything, I could be in real danger.

What am I going to do?

What am I going to tell him?

Think of something, Michael . . . think!

I let my hands slide off the table edge and uttered a loud groan.

I rolled my eyes up in my head. Tilted my body ... tilted ...

... until I fell off the chair, onto my side on the carpet.

"Ow!"

I landed harder than I had planned.

Above me, I heard General Rameer cry out in surprise. I saw two servants come hurrying over to see what the problem was.

General Rameer climbed out of his chair and leaned over me. He gazed down with real concern. He shook me gently with both hands. "Michael? Are you okay?"

I groaned again and rolled onto my back. I blinked several times.

"Sorry," I whispered. "I — I'm okay."

I sat up unsteadily, blinking a few more times.

General Rameer stepped back. He let out a sigh of relief. The color came back to his face.

"It's all . . . too big a shock," I said, rubbing my forehead. "I mean . . . yesterday I was a kid from Long Island. Flying to meet my aunt and going to Disney World. And today . . ."

"Yes, yes." The general helped me gently to my feet. "I understand."

He held onto me until he was sure I was steady. "You have had your whole world turned upside down, Excellency. I am so sorry. I didn't mean to hurry you. It is just that we must have Pukrah and the sapphire back — immediately."

"Yes. Of course," I replied, swallowing.

He handed me the water goblet. "I will give you time to rest. And to think. Later, once you are feeling better, we will talk again."

I nodded weakly and took a long drink. Two uniformed guards appeared from out of nowhere. General Rameer ordered them to take me to my quarters.

They led me down an endless hallway. The walls were covered in silky gold curtains. I gazed at a long row of enormous, gold-framed oil paintings. Portraits of old-fashioned-looking people, all dark and short and kind of chubby.

Are these really my ancestors? I wondered.

No. I was sure that General Rameer and his

men made a terrible mistake. They got the wrong boy, I decided. It's as simple as that.

And that note from my parents? Just a joke? Or did my parents somehow make the same mistake?

It was all too much to think about. I felt as if my head was bursting!

The guards led me to my quarters — not just one room, but several huge rooms around an outdoor courtyard with a tall, bubbling fountain.

I stepped into the front room, all gold and silver and red. The room was as big as my whole house back home. Filled with chairs and couches and desks and bookshelves, and furniture I didn't even recognize!

I didn't really get a good look. Because my eyes stopped at the telephone on the desk against the back wall.

And I knew instantly what I had to do.

I had to call Mom and Dad back home. I had to get a call through to New York. I had to explain the mistake that had been made.

They must be so frantic, so worried, I realized. When Aunt Sandra called them and told them I didn't arrive in Orlando, they probably went nuts. They must have the police and the FBI out looking for me!

My heart pounding, I practically leaped across the enormous room. I grabbed the phone.

Mom and Dad will know how to get me away from here, I told myself. They'll talk to this general. And I'll be on the first plane back to New York.

I lifted the receiver to my ear and listened for the buzz of a dial tone.

Instead, I heard silence. A click.

Then a man's voice purred in my ear: "Yes, Excellency? Did you wish to make a call?"

I groaned. "Are you the . . . operator?"

"Yes, I am *your* operator," he replied.

"Well . . . I'd like to call Long Island, New York," I told him, trying to sound calm.

"I'm so sorry," he said. "I cannot make that call."

"Excuse me?" I cried. "You mean —"

"I have certain orders, Excellency."

"But — but —"

"I'm really sorry, sir. Do you wish to call somewhere else?"

"Uh . . . yes," I replied, thinking quickly. "I'd like to call Orlando. Orlando, Florida."

"Oh, I'm sorry, Excellency. I cannot do that."

"But I need to speak to my aunt!" I shouted angrily, losing it.

"I'm so sorry," he purred. "My orders, sir."

"Orders?" I shrieked. "What exactly are your orders?"

"From the general," he replied, softly, calmly. "You're not allowed to make any calls. Until the general gives permission."

I slammed down the receiver.

I glanced quickly around the room. Now what?

I have to get out of the palace, I decided. If I can get away from here and get into town, I can use a pay phone, a phone *without* a personal operator!

It shouldn't be too hard to sneak away, I told myself. I just have to avoid the guards.

I took a deep breath and trotted to the door.

My hand trembled as I grabbed the shiny brass knob. Turned it. Pulled.

The door wouldn't move.

I tried pushing. Then pulling.

"Excellency?" a voice called from the other side of the door. "Is there anything I can get you?"

A guard.

I was locked inside. And the door was guarded. General Rameer wasn't taking any chances.

"Doesn't he *trust* me?" I murmured out loud.

I'm trapped here, I realized. I'm supposed to be their ruler — but I'm a prisoner until I lead them to Pukrah's mummy.

With a heavy sigh, I threw myself onto one of the red velvet couches. I sank into the cushion and buried my face in my hands.

A few seconds later, I heard a cough.

The rustle of a curtain.

A footstep.

I'm not alone in here, I realized.

I lowered my hands from my face and spun around.

"Who's there?"

girl about my age stepped out from behind the silk curtains.

She was tall and thin, dressed in a white polo shirt tucked into white shorts. She had short red-brown hair parted in the middle, with bangs that came down to her olive-colored eyes.

"Who are you?" I cried, jumping to my feet.

She raised a finger to her lips. "Shhh." Her green eyes flashed. She motioned to the door. "They will hear," she whispered.

She tiptoed over the thick carpet, studying me as she walked. "Are you the prince?"

"I — I guess," I stammered. "But who are you?"

She returned her finger to her lips. "Shhh. The guards don't know I'm in here. I'm Megan Kerr."

"Michael Clarke," I told her. "At least, I *thought*

I was Michael Clarke until this morning. Now I'm not really sure what my name is."

She studied me some more. "Is it okay to call you Michael?"

I shrugged. "Whatever."

"Should I call you Excellency?"

"No — please!" I begged.

Her eyes went to the door. We could hear two guards talking on the other side.

"Well, who *are* you?" I demanded. "What are you doing in here? You don't sound like you're from here. Are you an American?"

She pulled me over to the red velvet couch. I sat down next to her.

"Yes, I'm American," she whispered. Her expression turned solemn. "My parents were the American advisers to General Rameer. They were both killed in a bomb explosion."

"I'm sorry," I whispered.

She twisted a strand of her bangs between her fingers, then let go and dropped her hand to her lap. She sighed. "I had no relatives back home. Nowhere to go. No one to take me. So General Rameer adopted me."

"You live in the palace?" I asked.

She nodded.

"What's it like?" I whispered.

"It's *horrible*!" she replied. "I miss my friends. There are no other kids here. I miss my school. I miss everything! And look at this place."

She swept her hand around. "It's all so fancy. Everything is gold and silver. Jeweled this and velvet that and silk that! Nothing is normal! I can't put a poster up in my room. I can't get any good CD's. I can't —"

She realized she had raised her voice. She gasped. We both turned to the door.

"I'm sorry. Why are we talking about me?" she whispered. "*You* are the one who is in trouble."

Her words sent a chill down the back of my neck. "Yes, I know. I'm in major trouble."

She leaned closer. Her eyes burned into mine. "You don't know, Michael. You don't have any idea how much trouble you're in."

"Huh? What do you mean?"

"These are bad men," Megan whispered.

"But, Megan, General Rameer is your father now. He adopted you —" I protested.

She shut her eyes. "I don't care. He is the most evil of all of them. They are bad men, Michael."

She opened her eyes and turned to me. Her chin trembled. "Do you really think General Rameer is going to let *you* rule the kingdom?"

I swallowed. "I don't understand. . . ."

"General Rameer has fought a war for twelve years," she explained. "Now that he has nearly won, he will not give up his power to a twelve-year-old."

"But he calls me Excellency," I argued. "And he

said that once I have showed him the hiding place of the mummy —"

"After you lead them to the mummy, they plan to *kill* you!" Megan cried.

My mouth dropped open in horror.

"That is why I sneaked in here," Megan whispered. "To warn you."

"But I don't even know where the mummy is!" I exclaimed.

Megan's eyes narrowed. "Then you are in even bigger trouble," she said. "They will torture you. They —"

The door burst open.

Two brown-uniformed guards leaped into the room.

Megan and I jumped to our feet.

Before Megan could take a step, the guards grabbed her.

"Let *go* of me!" she screamed, trying to twist free. "Let go!"

They dragged her to the door.

"Where are you taking her?" I cried. "What are you going to do to her?"

The door slammed behind them.

I could hear Megan arguing with the guards, telling them to let her go, all the way down the long hall.

I froze in place, waiting for my heart to stop racing. I stared at the door, as if expecting it to burst open again, for the guards to return and drag me away too.

"What am I going to do?" I asked myself out loud.

Megan's frightening words repeated in my ears. *They are evil men. . . . They plan to kill you. . . . They will torture you.*

But if they have the wrong kid . . . I told myself, my thoughts whirring frantically through my mind.

If they have the wrong kid, they'll *have* to let me go — right?

They can't keep me here if I'm not the baby that was sent to America twelve years ago.

Maybe I *am* that baby, I argued with myself.

But if I am that baby and the memory chip was planted in my brain . . . *why don't I remember?*

Stop! I ordered myself. I shook my head hard, trying to stop all these desperate thoughts.

I stared at the door.

"Whoa." I realized the two guards weren't out there. They had dragged Megan away.

Was it possible? Did they leave the door unlocked?

I took off. Leaped over a red armchair and flew to the door. I grabbed the knob. Turned it — and pulled.

Yes!

The door swung open.

I poked my head into the hall, expecting to see guards.

I peered in both directions. Empty. The long golden-walled hallway stood empty as far as I could see.

I stepped out, my heart pounding so hard I could feel it against my ribs.

I carefully closed the door behind me.

Which way? Which way?

I had to find the back of the palace. Maybe

there were fewer guards there, I decided. Maybe if I could get to the back, I stood a chance of escaping.

Shafts of yellow sunlight streamed through the tall windows that lined the hall. It was still morning, so the sun was still in the east, I figured.

But what direction did the palace face?

I didn't have a clue.

Get going, Michael, I ordered myself. The important thing is to get *out* of here!

Keeping against the wall, I began jogging to my right. My shoes thudded softly over the thick red carpet.

Sunlight flooded the hall. The tall windows stretched nearly from floor to ceiling. Between the windows, big oil portraits of my ancestors — or *somebody's* ancestors — stared down at me, watching me run.

Near the end of the hall, silky gold curtains billowed in a soft breeze, making a scraping sound over the carpet.

I was nearly to the curtains when I heard another sound. The thud of footsteps.

"Oh!" A sharp cry escaped my throat.

I dove behind the curtains. Pulled them around me. Dropped to my knees. Peered out the side.

Several guards marched past, rifles held stiffly in front of them. They moved in a tight formation, eyes straight ahead, swinging their free arms in a steady rhythm, not saying a word.

I held my breath until they turned a corner. Then, slowly, shakily, I climbed to my feet.

A close call, I told myself.

Now what? Which direction do I go?

My legs trembled as I stepped out from behind the curtains. Silence in the hall now.

And then I heard a *PING PING*.

What's making that sound?

I turned and saw an enormous insect — some kind of giant horsefly maybe — flying into a windowpane.

PING . . . PING . . .

The insect kept flying at the window, wings fluttering furiously, battering its fat black body against the glass.

What a waste of time, I thought. It'll never get out the window that way.

PING PING.

I watched the big insect try again, again.

Out the window, I thought. Out the window . . .

Yes!

Maybe I can escape out the window.

I dove across the hall. I brushed the big, buzzing insect away with one hand. And stepped up to the window.

It was a double window with a handle on each pane.

I peered out, into a large, grassy courtyard. Empty. Guarded only by a tall granite statue of some kind of winged person.

43

No human guards.

Excellent!

I grabbed the window handles, one in each hand. And I tugged.

The windows were heavier than I thought. They didn't budge.

I squeezed the metal handles and tugged harder.

Please open, I prayed. *Please . . . please . . .*

Yes! The windows began to move. As I pulled, they slid toward me, creaking heavily.

Yes!

I pulled them open just wide enough to slip through.

Warm, fresh air from the courtyard greeted me.

I leaned out. Pressed my hands on the window ledge. Started to lift myself up. Up and out . . .

And felt strong hands grab my shoulders.

"Yaaaaii!" A startled scream burst from my throat.

The hands tightened, pulled me back in.

I turned to face two grim-looking guards.

"General Rameer will not like this," one of them said, frowning.

"Come with us," his partner ordered. And then he added with a sneer, "Excellency."

10

The two guards led me down a flight of marble stairs. We passed several meeting rooms with long mahogany tables. Then a library with bookshelves covering the walls and a pool table in the middle of the room.

We passed a kitchen where several white-uniformed cooks busily prepared lunch. The smell of fried onions followed us down the hall.

We turned a corner and entered a small room. As I stepped inside, I saw that all four walls were covered with maps. Most of them, I guessed, were close-up, detailed maps of Jezekiah and its neighbors.

Some of the maps were covered with red and blue pins. Some maps had been scrawled on, with lines and circles drawn in red and blue ink.

General Rameer sat at a desk at the back of the

room. He had a large map unrolled on the desktop. He leaned over it, scowling and murmuring to himself, drawing a line on the map with one finger.

He glanced up quickly when he heard the guards and me enter. "Michael?" His features twisted in confusion.

"He was trying to escape from the palace," one of the guards reported.

General Rameer narrowed his eyes at me. "Where?" he asked the guards. "How was he trying to escape?"

"Through windows leading to the east portico," a guard reported.

General Rameer scowled at me, furrowing his white brows sternly. "You may leave us," he told the guards, waving both hands, motioning for them to go. "Wait outside the door."

The guards turned and walked out stiffly. They closed the door behind them.

General Rameer squinted at me, tapping his big green ring on top of the map on his desk.

I stood awkwardly in the middle of the room, clasping and unclasping my fists. My heart thudded in my chest. It felt like that big horsefly was inside me — *PING PING* — banging against my insides, trying to break out.

"You know the palace is heavily guarded?" the general asked finally.

I nodded. "Yeah. I know," I murmured in a hoarse, frightened voice.

"And you still tried to escape through a window?"

"Yeah," I confessed. "I tried."

His laugh startled me, made me jump.

"That's just the kind of bravery we expect from our leader!" he declared. He stepped around the desk and clapped me hard on the back. He shook my hand, squeezing it till my knuckles cracked.

"I knew you were the right boy, Michael," he said, smiling warmly, his white teeth gleaming under the low ceiling lights. "The ruler of this kingdom has to have that kind of reckless courage."

"Uh . . . yeah. I guess," I replied weakly.

My legs were shaking. I didn't know what to say. I could barely think straight!

He rested a hand heavily on my shoulder and guided me to the wall across from the desk. "Come look at this map," he said, still smiling.

He pointed his walking stick over a large color map of Jezekiah, mostly oranges and yellows. Across the desert in black were crude line drawings of structures. Maybe caves or lakes or something.

"This is your kingdom," General Rameer said. He stabbed a finger onto a black star near the southern border. "This is the palace right here. We are in the capital city of Ramenn."

He pulled his finger away, and I stared at the

star as if I could actually see the palace and the town.

"Did you study Jezekiah in school?" he asked.

"Well . . . no," I replied honestly.

He frowned. "We will have to make the kingdom more well known, won't we?" he declared. "We will have to put Jezekiah on the map, so to speak."

"I guess," I replied weakly.

"Here is the desert," the general continued, sliding his stick over the large orange-yellow area. "As you can see, most of the kingdom is desert. And the desert is filled with many tall rock structures. And cut into these tall rocks are many caves."

He turned to make sure I was concentrating. I stared straight ahead at the map.

"Go ahead, Michael. Take a good look at the caves," he urged, lowering his voice. He took a step back so that I could see the entire map.

"Go ahead," he repeated, his hand heavily on my shoulder again.

My eyes swept over the drawings on the yellow map. I saw dozens of caves, some big, some little.

Why is he showing me this? I asked myself. Why is he making me study the caves?

Of course, I knew the answer.

I knew what was coming next. And it filled me with cold dread.

"Which cave is it, Michael?" General Rameer

asked softly, tightening his hand on my shoulder. "Which cave is Pukrah's mummy hidden in?"

I stared straight ahead at the map.

I realized I was breathing hard, my chest heaving up and down.

"Which cave?" General Rameer repeated. "You have the information in your brain, Michael. Point to it now. Show me the hiding place of Pukrah's mummy."

"I . . . I . . ."

My knees were trembling so hard, they were knocking together.

I turned to the general. "I can't remember!" I cried. "Really. I'm telling you the truth, General Rameer! I really can't remember!"

General Rameer's smile didn't fade. "That's no problem, Michael," he said softly. "No problem at all."

"Wh-what do you mean?" I stammered.

"Well . . . the memory chip is in your brain, right?" He tightened his grip on my shoulder. "We'll just have our doctors cut open your brain and remove the chip."

he guards ushered me back to my room. They practically had to carry me. My legs felt weak and wobbly and I could barely force them to move.

I slumped into the room and they closed the door behind me. I heard a key turn the lock and knew I was a prisoner once again.

"Aaaagh!" I uttered an angry cry and heaved a velvet throw pillow across the room. It bounced off a silky window curtain and dropped to the carpet.

I lifted a glass vase off the desk and raised it over my head. I felt like smashing everything. I wanted to trash the room, break everything, destroy it all.

I set the vase back down and started to pace the room furiously. I felt angry and terrified at the same time.

"What am I going to do?" I asked myself out loud.

I can't let them cut open my brain. I can't let them operate on me.

I stopped suddenly, grabbing the back of the red couch. I had a sudden flash.

"Megan — are you here?" I called. "Are you back? Are you hiding in here?"

Silence.

"Megan?"

No. Not here.

I was suddenly afraid for her too. The guards had dragged her away when they caught her trying to help me. What had they done to her?

She was General Rameer's daughter now. He wouldn't harm her — would he?

Several hard raps on the door made me jump.

The door swung open and Lieutenant Henry swept in, his ponytail flying behind him. He wore the same outfit as on the plane — a green-and-black camouflage jacket over baggy khakis.

His dark eyes glanced around the room, then settled on me. "Excellency," he said, bowing his tanned head slightly. "Pardon the intrusion."

I just stared at him. I didn't know how to reply.

"General Rameer sent me to speak to you," Lieutenant Henry said. "He wishes for there to be no trouble."

"Me too," I murmured. I dropped onto the arm of the couch with a sigh.

"We only ask you to restore the pride of our nation," Lieutenant Henry continued, speaking emotionally, gesturing with both hands.

"All of our people will rejoice when the mummy of Pukrah is restored to its place in the palace, along with the sapphire."

He paused, expecting me to say something. But again, I just stared back.

"You will make so many people happy by revealing the mummy's hiding place," Lieutenant Henry continued. "Why do you hesitate, Excellency? Why do you make things difficult for everyone?"

I jumped to my feet. "I'm not trying to make things difficult!" I cried. "I'm telling the truth. I don't remember anything about Pukrah's mummy. I don't *know* anything!"

Lieutenant Henry nodded and made a clicking sound with his tongue and teeth. "Too bad," he said softly. He waved to the door.

Two brown-uniformed guards stepped into the room.

"Take the boy to surgery," Lieutenant Henry ordered.

I struggled to escape them. I twisted and squirmed and kicked.

But it was no use.

They forced me to change into a paper surgical

robe. A few minutes later, I was lying on my back, strapped down to a metal stretcher.

Four guards wheeled me into an operating room in the basement of the palace. Blinding bright lights flashed on overhead.

Blinking, I stared up at two doctors and a nurse, all in white surgical gowns, white masks over their mouths and noses.

"The operation will be simple," one of the doctors announced. He grabbed my head in one hand, the way you'd pick up a melon from a grocery shelf.

"We will cut like this," he said. He scraped his finger along the top of my head. "One long slice. Then we saw open the skull to get to the brain."

"Please hurry," I heard a familiar voice say from somewhere behind me. General Rameer's voice, low and calm. "The whole nation is waiting for that memory chip."

The other doctor raised a black rubber mask over my head. "First we will put you to sleep," he said, leaning over me. "When I place this over your mouth and nose, begin taking deep breaths."

He began to lower the mask.

"No — wait!" I screamed. "Wait — please! I remember now! It all just came back to me! Please — stop! I remember everything!"

12

"**W**ait!" I heard General Rameer's cry from the back of the operating room.

The doctors stepped aside, and the general leaned over me. He stared hard at me, biting his bottom lip, trying to decide if I was telling the truth. He scratched his white curly hair, studying my face.

"Your memory came back to you, Michael?" he asked finally.

"Yes!" I cried. "Everything. It — it was like someone turned a switch."

General Rameer turned to the doctors. "Unstrap him from the table. The guards will bring him to me in the map room."

"Should he change into his clothes?" one of the doctors asked.

General Rameer frowned. "No. Leave him in the operating gown. Just in case . . ."

A few minutes later, I stood in the little basement room surrounded by wall maps.

General Rameer stepped to my side. His walking stick clicked on the floor. He eyed me suspiciously.

"I am so glad your memory returned, Michael," he said. "The operation would be painful for you. It would take you many months to recover."

I took a deep breath. His words sent a sharp pain shooting through my head. I imagined a knife cutting through my brain.

"Yeah. I'm glad too," I murmured, avoiding his probing eyes. "It all just came back to me — in a flash."

"Very good, very good," he muttered.

He guided me to the orange-and-yellow wall map we had studied that morning. "Okay, here we are," he said, moving the tip of the stick across the star that marked the Royal Palace.

"Show me, Michael. Show me what you remember. Where will we find the sacred mummy and its hidden jewel?"

I turned to the map. My eyes swept over the desert and its dozens of rock cliffs and caves.

I couldn't focus. I was too frightened. They were all a blur to me.

"Can you find the mummy's hiding place on this

map?" General Rameer urged. "Can you point to the location, Michael?" I could hear the impatience growing in his voice.

"Well . . ." I ran my hand over the middle of the map.

A wave of panic swept over me. My heart raced. I struggled to keep breathing normally. But my throat was so tight, I made a wheezing sound with each breath.

What am I going to do? I asked myself.

I don't have a clue about the mummy's hiding place.

I don't know *anything*.

But I can't let them cut into my brain. I can't!

I'll stall him, I decided. I'll pick a cave that's really far away. And then . . .

Then . . .

Maybe I can escape before he finds out it's a wild goose chase.

Wild goose chase. That was one of my dad's expressions. He said that all the time.

I pictured Mom and Dad back home in Long Island.

Then I remembered that they may not be my mom and dad.

"Michael? I'm waiting." General Rameer's voice broke into my troubled thoughts.

"Uh . . . yeah."

I pointed to a cave way down at the bottom of the map. "Pukrah's mummy is hidden in the back of this cave," I told him, trying to keep my voice from trembling.

The general narrowed his eyes at me. Studied my face for a long moment.

I turned away and concentrated on the map. My chin started to tremble. I covered it with one hand.

"The mummy is . . . uh . . . hidden behind a wall of stones," I added.

Very good, Michael, I congratulated myself.

That's a nice detail. It makes it sound as if you really know what you are talking about.

General Rameer leaned forward. He brought his face inches from the map and squinted at the cave I had picked.

After a few seconds, he straightened up. "That cave is the hiding place? You are sure?"

My whole body trembled. I hoped he couldn't see it.

I nodded. "Yes. That's the one."

"Very good." A smile crossed General Rameer's face. He placed a hand on my shoulder. "We will leave first thing in the morning. You will lead the way."

13

I couldn't get to sleep that night. I was lying in bed, staring up at the ceiling. A thousand horrifying thoughts raced through my mind.

Moonlight from the window fell on the tall grandfather's clock against the wall. The clock read 2:00 A.M.

I heard a stirring sound. Soft thuds.

And a hand tightened over my mouth.

Kicking, thrashing, I struggled to sit up.

The bed table light flashed on. And I stared up at Megan.

She raised a finger to her lips. And slowly took her hand from over my mouth. "Ssshhh."

"You scared me to death!" I wheezed. "How — how did you get in?"

Her green eyes flashed in the yellow light. She

tossed her bangs away from her eyes. "Don't make a sound, Michael," she warned. "There are *four* guards outside your door tonight. And they are all awake and alert."

I sat up against the headboard and straightened my pajama shirt. "What did they do to you?" I whispered. "I mean, after they caught you in here with me?"

"They didn't do anything," she replied. "I'm the general's adopted daughter — remember?"

I nodded.

She dropped down beside me on the edge of the bed. She was dressed entirely in black — black tank top, black skirt over black tights.

"I came to warn you," she whispered. "Did you tell the general the true hiding place? I hope so."

I stared at her. I didn't know what to say. Should I tell her the truth?

She didn't wait for me to reply. "I hope you told the truth, Michael. These men are desperate — and very cruel. If you lied to them . . ." Her voice trailed off.

A noise at the window made us both gasp.

Another large insect bumping the glass.

Megan's eyes locked on mine. "Did they tell you about the curse, Michael?"

"Huh? Curse?" I choked out.

"General Rameer and his men are so superstitious," Megan whispered. "They were probably too superstitious to tell you about the curse."

"Tell me," I insisted.

"The mummy of Pukrah belongs to the people of Jezekiah," she explained. "It is said that if Pukrah falls into the wrong hands . . . if his mummy falls into evil hands . . . Pukrah will walk! Pukrah will walk the earth until the evil is destroyed."

"Wow," I murmured.

"The men are all superstitious, Michael," she continued. "Sure, they want to own the jewel hidden inside the mummy. But mainly, they want the ancient mummy. They are so superstitious! They don't believe they can rule the kingdom unless they own the mummy.

"It is totally important to them," Megan continued. "So if you are trying to fool them . . ."

I let out a long sigh. Could I tell her the truth? Could I tell her my horrible secret?

No, I decided.

No.

I think I can trust her. But I don't want to get her into trouble with her new father. I'd better not share my secret with her.

"Everything's . . . fine," I said. But my voice cracked as I said it.

She stared at me. "Yes?"

"Yes," I insisted. "The memory chip — it clicked in. Really. All of a sudden, I remembered everything."

She continued to stare at me, studying me.

"I looked at that map, and it suddenly became so

60

familiar," I continued. "I knew the right cave as soon as I saw it."

A smile spread over her face. "Michael — that's great!" she cried.

"Yeah. Right," I agreed.

Did she believe me? Yes. I was sure that she did.

"I was so worried about you!" she cried. "I — I didn't want anything to happen to you!"

"No problem," I assured her.

Her smile grew even wider. "I'll be coming along tomorrow," she declared. "It'll be so *exciting*!"

She moved quickly to the window. "See you in the morning," she whispered.

And then she silently disappeared out the window, leaving the curtains fluttering.

"Yeah, *exciting*, for sure," I muttered, rolling my eyes. "It's going to be *real* exciting."

I knew that Megan was only trying to help me. But her stories about how cruel and desperate General Rameer's men were did not help calm me down.

And I knew the story about Pukrah's curse would give me nightmares for years to come — *if* I lived that long!

If I lived past tomorrow . . .

What will they do to me when we get to the cave and the mummy isn't there? I wondered. What will they do when they learn I was lying?

Kill me on the spot?

Drag me back to the palace, remove the memory chip from my brain — and *then* kill me?

Why wasn't the memory chip working?

Because I'm the wrong boy? Because I'm not the son of the kingdom's rulers? Because a horrible mistake has been made?

These questions repeated and repeated until I felt my brain about to explode!

I lay trembling under the covers, staring up at the ceiling, thinking . . . thinking.

I didn't sleep for a moment. I was still wide awake, questions rolling through my mind, when the guards came in to awaken me.

They handed me a green-and-black camouflage suit.

"Excellency, you are to get dressed," one of them instructed. "We leave at dawn."

I stood up, stretching, and peered out the window. In the far distance, I saw a thin line of red, the sun beginning to rise at the horizon.

I'm doomed, I realized.

Doomed.

gulped down a quick breakfast of toast and orange juice. Then the guards led me outside.

A red ball of a sun still hung low on the horizon. It cast a rosy glow over the dozens and dozens of people scurrying around, over soldiers, palace guards, servants.

An endless line of Jeeps and army trucks jammed the road outside the palace. I watched armed soldiers hoisting themselves into the backs of olive-colored troop vans. Servants loaded piles of supplies into smaller trucks.

Whistles blew. I saw Lieutenant Henry in the middle of the road, shouting instructions.

The guards led me through the crowd to the Jeep at the head of the line. Megan stood at the side of the Jeep, wearing a brown-and-green camouflage suit and a brown beret tilted over her hair.

She greeted me with a nod. "Good morning, Excellency," she said. Her eyes were on the guards at my sides.

"No, it isn't," I whispered. I motioned behind me. "I thought we were going on a mummy hunt," I said. "Why is General Rameer bringing along all these soldiers?"

"For safety," Megan replied. She pointed to the desert. "There are still many rebel soldiers out there. They haven't given up. The war continues."

"Oh, great," I groaned. "Something *else* to worry about!"

General Rameer appeared, wearing a brown army uniform, the jacket chest covered with sparkling medals. He clapped me on the back. "A great day!" he declared happily. "A great day for the kingdom of Jezekiah! At last, our national treasure will be back to where it belongs!"

Megan and I exchanged glances.

General Rameer motioned for us to climb into the Jeep. Megan sat up front with the driver. The general and I sat together in the back.

"How long does it take to get to the cave?" I asked him.

He unfolded a map and stretched it across his lap. "We should be there by nightfall," he replied. He turned to me with a smile. "It is a small kingdom, Michael. It only looks big on this map. You can travel anywhere in Jezekiah in one day."

One day to live, I thought. I have one day to live.

The general was staring at me. I forced a smile to my face. I didn't want to let him see how frightened I was.

A van filled with soldiers pulled in front of our Jeep. Two other vans moved to our sides.

We were surrounded by armed men. Their job, I realized, was to protect the general — and me — from rebel attack.

General Rameer stood up in the back of our Jeep and swept his walking stick forward, a signal to move out. A few seconds later, we began to move, slowly at first, then picking up speed on the narrow paved road that led through the desert.

The sun was high in the sky now, and the air grew hot. The road ended after only a few miles, and the Jeep bounced over sand and rock.

General Rameer studied his map, shouting directions to the driver. I gazed out at the desert that surrounded us.

White rock and yellow sand as far as I could see.

I suddenly felt as if I were on another planet. This must be what it's like to ride over the surface of the moon, I thought.

Ahead of us, swirls of wind sent sheets of sand rolling over the ground like dry ocean waves. On all sides, tall white rock formations rose up like small mountains.

We passed a tiny, round pool of blue water surrounded by low-leaning palm trees. It looked like a movie set. It didn't look real.

Beyond the pool, a deep shadow fell over the sand. The shadow of a high rock cliff, dark caves cut into the bottom.

Ugly black-and-white desert birds, tall and scrawny, perched on the rocks. They stood perfectly still, staring down at us as we rumbled past.

The sunlight made the swirling sand sparkle like gold. Tall white granite cliffs gleamed ahead of us.

Strange, beautiful scenery. But of course I couldn't enjoy any of it.

I knew that every minute in the desert was bringing me closer to my doom.

Every cave we passed, every rock formation, made me shudder.

There's no escape, I realized. There's nowhere out here to run.

By tonight, General Rameer will know the truth. The mummy will still be hidden. Everyone will know that I lied, that I led them all to the farthest cave because I didn't know what else to do.

We stopped for lunch at a flat area surrounded by low rocks.

I pulled Megan aside. I was desperate to talk to her.

"Do you have any ideas?" I demanded. "What am I going to do?"

She squinted at me as if she didn't know what I was talking about. "I don't know how I can help you, Excellency," she replied loudly.

"Huh? Megan?"

I turned and saw my two guards behind me. Listening to every word.

No way I could talk to Megan.

I choked down a sandwich. I don't know how I swallowed it. My throat was dry as sand, my stomach knotted, rumbling.

I gazed up at the scrawny black-and-white birds perched above us on the rocks. Were they desert vultures?

Would they be feasting on *me* tonight?

After a few minutes, the journey began again. General Rameer studied his map. He became more and more excited as we bounced over the sand, riding nearer and nearer to the cave at the bottom of the map.

The longest afternoon of my life!

I felt sick. Sweat rolled down my forehead, into my eyes. I didn't even brush it away.

I tried to think. Tried to come up with a plan.

But my mind was as empty as the cave I had picked!

Could I tell General Rameer that I made a mistake? Could I point to another cave on the map — a cave clear on the other side of the desert?

It might give me an extra day to live, I thought. But, no. No way he would buy that story.

He would know instantly that I was stalling. That I was a total phony and a liar.

The sun was lowering itself behind tall rock cliffs when we suddenly stopped.

General Rameer folded up his map. He tapped the knee of my camouflage pants with his walking stick. "That's it!" he cried, pointing excitedly. "That's the cave!"

I gazed up at the tall rock cliff. It jutted straight up from the sand, glowing blue in the evening light. At its bottom, a dark cave opening, shaped almost like those mouse holes in the cartoons.

General Rameer jumped down from the Jeep. He motioned for me to join him.

I climbed out slowly, breathing hard, my heart pounding.

I brushed sand from my eyes.

"The big moment!" General Rameer declared, gazing up at the cave opening.

I can't do this, I thought. I can't go through with this.

I'm going crazy. I can't take it for another second!

"General Rameer, I — I have to tell you something," I started. The words caught in my throat. I coughed. Forced myself to continue.

I had no choice. I had to tell him the truth.

"General Rameer, I was lying," I confessed. "I

was stalling. I don't remember anything. I don't *know* anything. I'm sorry — but I don't have a clue about where the mummy is."

Somehow I got those words out. With a long sigh, I took a step back.

And watched General Rameer's face turn red and his eyes bulge wide in fury.

Please —" I started. "I didn't mean —"

It took me a few seconds to realize that the general wasn't staring at me.

And he hadn't heard a word I said.

"Michael — get down!" he cried. He shoved me to the ground beside the Jeep.

I heard a loud *CRAACK CRAACK*.

Firecrackers, I thought.

Then I realized it was gunfire.

A *CRAACK* very close — followed by the whoosh of air escaping one of the Jeep tires.

"Rebels!" I heard Lieutenant Henry shout. "They're up high — on the cliff! Can't tell how many!"

I raised my eyes to the cliff and saw black-uniformed soldiers firing down at us. Behind me,

General Rameer's soldiers came piling out of vans, raising their weapons into position.

"Get to that rock!" General Rameer ordered me, pointing to a wide boulder rising up from the sand. "Go!" He pulled me to my feet and gave me a hard shove.

I saw Megan duck down on the other side of the Jeep.

More gunfire. General Rameer's men began firing back. General Rameer tossed his stick away, pulled an assault rifle from a supply van, turned, raised it onto his shoulder, and fired it up at the high cliffs.

The crack and whistle of bullets rang out over the sand, echoed off the tall rocks.

Birds flew crazily overhead. The sky darkened as a heavy cloud rolled in.

Soldiers ran toward the rocks, firing their weapons up at the black-uniformed rebels.

Shouts rang out over the rifle fire.

I dove to the boulder and scrambled behind it on my hands and knees.

This is *horrible*! I told myself, gripping the side of the rock, pressing myself against it. A war. A real war — and I'm in the middle of it.

I heard a scream of pain. Furious shouts.

People are getting hurt, I realized. Maybe killed.

I've got to get away. . . .

Get away?

My heart skipped a beat. Yes!

This is my chance, I decided. My chance to escape from General Rameer, to escape from Jezekiah.

I glanced behind me. Nothing but blue sand, the desert darkening as night fell.

Where will I go?

I remembered seeing small towns on the map, small towns on the other side of the Jezekiah border.

If I can get away without being seen, I can hide in a cave or behind some rocks, I decided.

Then tomorrow morning I can head for the border and find one of those small towns.

It was a crazy, desperate idea.

But it just might save my life.

I took one last peek over the boulder. General Rameer and his soldiers were running up the side of the rock cliff, weapons roaring.

I looked for Megan, but I couldn't find her.

"Bye, everyone," I murmured.

I spun away from the boulder — and took off over the sand.

16

My shoes crunched over the hard packed sand. My shadow stretched in front of me as if leading the way.

I had run about ten or twelve steps when the shooting stopped.

My heavy footsteps suddenly sounded so loud!

"Excellency — where are you going?" a voice shouted.

Gasping, panting hard, I spun around — and saw Lieutenant Henry trotting after me. His ponytail bounced behind him as he ran. He held his rifle with one hand and motioned to me with the other.

"I — I —" I stammered, thinking hard, trying to come up with a good explanation.

"Do not be afraid, Excellency," Lieutenant

Henry said, stepping up to me. "It is over. The rebels have fled."

He jabbed his rifle toward the rock cliff. "See? They are gone. They never fight for long. A few shots — then they run."

I heard laughter from the rocks. I saw soldiers tossing their hats in the air. Congratulating each other. Celebrating their quick victory.

The victory was *too* quick, I thought unhappily, as I followed Lieutenant Henry back.

With a little more time, I might have escaped.

Two men had been wounded in the battle. They lay moaning on their backs on the sand. Medical officers leaned over them, treating their wounds.

I stopped walking. My whole body shuddered.

I felt sick again. I took a deep breath and held it, trying not to puke.

These men are willing to give their lives, I thought. They are willing to die to get Pukrah's mummy back.

And what have I done?

Lied to them. Led them on a wild goose chase.

And now I am doomed, I realized. Now they will enter the cave and see that I tried to fool them.

I turned toward the cave opening. Dark and wide, it looked like a giant mouth, ready to swallow me.

"That was very foolish!" I heard General Rameer cry angrily.

I turned and saw him, red-faced, scowling, scolding Megan.

"I am sorry that you were caught in a battle," the general shouted. "But you have to be smarter than that!"

I stepped up beside them. Megan frowned at me, then glanced away.

"What's wrong?" I asked.

General Rameer pointed at her disgustedly. "She hid under the Jeep."

"I just wanted to be safe!" Megan cried.

"Under the Jeep is not safe! Not safe!" the general fumed. "If a bullet hits the gas tank, the Jeep explodes. I don't call that safe."

"S-sorry," Megan stammered, still avoiding his gaze.

"You were lucky, Megan," the general said softly. Then, to my surprise, he pulled her close and hugged her. "You were very lucky."

He really cares about her, I realized.

He would be so totally shocked if he knew that she tried to help me.

Now, no one can help me, I thought sadly. No one.

"Are we . . . going into the cave now?" I asked General Rameer. I tried to keep my voice steady. I tried to sound calm. But my voice came out shrill and high.

The general let go of Megan and turned to me. "No. We cannot enter the cave yet. We cannot view the sacred mummy until we purify ourselves."

"Uh . . . how long will that take?" I asked.

General Rameer laughed. "You are eager to see the mummy too, aren't you, Michael? Of course you are. As our future ruler, you too are eager to see the sacred mummy returned to the Royal Palace."

"Of course," I choked out. "But how long will it take to purify ourselves?"

He slapped me on the back. "Hours!" he declared. "We must purify ourselves in the sand, the pure, clean sand of our ancestors. If we view the mummy in an unclean state, Pukrah will take his revenge on us."

Wow, I thought. These people really *are* superstitious.

I was glad. It meant I wasn't going to be found out immediately.

I had one more night.

The soldiers began to chant. The purifying ritual had begun.

They chanted and sang in a language I didn't recognize. Then they stepped away from the rocks, out onto the flat sand.

General Rameer motioned for Megan and me to follow. We had to be purified too.

The sun had set. The air had grown cool. Megan and I copied what the soldiers did.

We all pulled off our shoes and slowly walked barefoot across the sand. The sand was still hot from the sun, hotter than the night air.

76

The chanting voices rose. The sound floated over the desert.

And as the soldiers chanted, they began to bury themselves in the sand.

Megan and I followed their lead. We scraped the sand around us, scraped it away with both hands.

We dug holes around ourselves. It took a long time.

And all the while, General Rameer and his soldiers and servants sang and chanted.

They stopped when we were buried up to our necks.

I turned and stared at the weird sight. Dozens of heads poking up from the sand in the night darkness.

"I don't feel too purified," Megan whispered. "Mainly, I feel itchy."

"The sand is so warm," I whispered back. "I think it feels good."

Lieutenant Henry scowled at us. We turned away from each other and remained silent.

I stared up at the mouth of the cave. I shuddered again.

The ceremony ended. Men went to work setting up canvas tents.

General Rameer motioned me into a tent beside his. "Get some sleep, Michael," he instructed. "Tomorrow will be a proud and exciting day."

I don't *think* so, I thought unhappily.

Proud? Definitely not.

Exciting? Well . . .

I found a sleeping bag waiting for me inside the tent. I set my shoes down and crawled into it. I didn't bother to get undressed.

I knew I wouldn't be able to sleep. Again.

I stared up at the canvas tent walls, trying not to think about the next morning. Trying not to think about anything. Listening to the heavy silence of the desert at night.

No wind. No animal sounds. No cars.

Real silence.

Can I sneak away? I wondered. Can I escape into the darkness?

I crawled out of the sleeping bag. I grabbed up my shoes.

On my knees, I pushed open the tent flap — and peered outside.

A line of small campfires sent a flickering orange light over the tents. And in the darting light, I saw soldiers. Guards standing in a circle around the entire camp. Rifles ready.

No. No escape.

I ducked back into the tent.

And waited for morning.

The sun was still a red haze low over the desert sand when I heard the call. "Excellency — time to wake. Pukrah awaits!"

My hands trembled as I struggled to tie my shoes.

I felt shaky and weak. I had trouble focusing my eyes.

My back itched. I was already sweating, even in the cool morning air.

But these were small problems, I knew. These were no big deal.

My *big* problem could be described in two words — *no mummy*.

"There you are!" General Rameer greeted me cheerfully as I stumbled out of the tent.

The morning sun cast a rosy color over the sand and sky. I squinted into the shimmering haze. I couldn't see where the sand ended and the sky began.

I took a deep breath.

It could be one of my last, I thought.

I turned to the rock cliff. The white rocks also reflected the rosy glow of the sun. Cut jaggedly into the rock, the dark cave mouth loomed ahead of me.

A wave of panic forced me to step back.

I can't go in there, I realized. I just can't do it.

I felt General Rameer's hand on my shoulder. "This way," he said softly. "The men are all waiting, Michael. You and I must go first. We must lead them to Pukrah."

I tried to choke out a reply, but no sound came out.

The general kept his hand on my shoulder and guided me forward.

I glanced back and saw the men lined up, two by two. The line stretched along the Jeeps and trucks and beyond, into the red sand.

The fires had all burned out. But the guards remained in a circle around the camp, rifles on their shoulders.

Lieutenant Henry lined up behind General Rameer and me. He smiled and flashed me a thumbs-up.

He won't be smiling in a few minutes, I thought glumly.

No one will.

General Rameer took such long, fast strides, I nearly had to jog to keep up. In a few minutes, the tall sheet of rock loomed over us.

We stepped up to the dark mouth of the cave at its bottom.

The air from inside the cave brushed against me, cool and damp. My skin tingled. Even though the climb to the cave mouth wasn't at all steep, I was panting as if I had climbed a mountain.

"Wait here," General Rameer whispered. He turned and waited for the men to gather behind us. Then he closed his eyes, bowed his head, and said a whispered prayer.

When it was finished, he opened his eyes and rubbed his hand on the stone of the cave edge. "Rub your hand there, Michael," he instructed. "All of us must touch the luck of the cave."

I obeyed his instruction. I rubbed my hand on the damp stone.

"Now we are ready to greet Pukrah!" General Rameer announced.

We stepped side by side into the cave opening. Darkness swept around me. A damp chill made me shiver.

Flashlights and halogen torches clicked on as the others entered behind us. Beams of light flashed and flickered over the cave floor and up the stone walls.

The cave was deeper than I imagined. And taller. I couldn't see the ceiling in the darkness.

"Your parents chose a good spot to hide the sacred mummy and its jewel," General Rameer said, keeping close beside me. Even though he spoke softly, his words echoed against the high cave walls.

"There is the stone wall!" I heard Lieutenant Henry declare.

"Huh?" I gasped.

Excited cries rang out all around me. Men swung their lights straight ahead.

I squinted into the light. And saw stones piled on top of each other. A wall of stones, maybe eight or nine feet tall, stretching nearly the width of the cave.

"Just as His Excellency described!" General Rameer cried happily. "Yes, Michael. This must be the wall that hides the mummy. Pukrah waits for us behind those stones."

Whooooa, I thought. I made up the stone wall. But there's a wall standing right there!

Lucky. But how much longer can my luck hold out?

A hush fell over the cave. It was nearly silent now, except for shoes scraping on the dusty cave floor. And somewhere near the back of the cave, the soft trickle of water.

The lights beamed onto the stone wall. Bright as day. I could see every stone.

"We can squeeze past the wall one at a time," a soldier called.

"Too slow. Tear down the wall!" General Rameer ordered.

The men moved forward. They began tearing

away the stones. Pulling them off the wall and rolling them to the side.

I stood frozen beside General Rameer. Squinting into the beams of light.

My legs trembled. My throat tightened until I had to force myself to breathe.

A breath . . . then another . . . then another.

I knew that each breath brought me closer to my doom.

The walls echoed with the *CLACK* and *THUD* of rocks tossed to the cave floor. The men worked silently, their faces somber.

The general stood beside me, hands pressed to the waist of his camouflage suit. An eager smile spread over his face as he watched the wall come down.

He didn't move. He didn't blink.

Neither did I.

And then a man's shrill cry made us both jump.

Stones tumbled in a noisy avalanche.

A large section of the wall suddenly fell.

The men rushed forward.

Now they will know the truth, I realized.

Now they will know that I lied, that I led them here for no reason.

I shut my eyes and prepared to meet my fate.

yes shut, I heard startled cries. Loud gasps.

"It is Pukrah!" someone shouted.

More cries rang out and echoed all around.

I opened my eyes. Yes!

My mouth dropped open in shock.

Yes! Yes!

The ancient mummy stood there behind the fallen wall. Stood upright.

Revealed in the dancing beams of yellow light. Its gray gauze ragged and torn. The heavily bandaged head slightly tilted.

Yes!

It stood behind the fallen stones. Stood with its slender, wrapped arms crossed over its chest.

"Pukrah! Pukrah!"

The men's chant rose up around the cave.

General Rameer beamed, his eyes flashing. I saw the glow of tears rolling down his cheeks.

Tears of joy.

"Pukrah! Pukrah!" the gleeful chant swelled.

The lights danced over the small, frail figure.

I let out a long, relieved sigh.

I knew this had to be the luckiest day of my life.

Somehow I had picked the right cave. Somehow I had pointed my finger blindly at some marks on a map — and I had found the mummy.

I suddenly felt so light, as if an enormous weight had been removed from my shoulders. I felt as if I could spread my arms and fly, fly to the roof of the cave!

I wanted to leap. I wanted to shout. I wanted to scream for joy.

But then, suddenly, the chanting stopped. The men grew silent.

I turned — and gasped.

I watched the mummy's frail, crossed arms unfold. The bandaged arms slowly slid down to its sides.

The small head tilted.

And then cries of horror rang out all around me as the mummy took a lurching step forward.

And then another.

"The mummy walks!" General Rameer cried. *"The mummy walks!"*

19

The mummy stuck out its arms stiffly and staggered forward. It scraped its gauzed feet over the cave floor, sending up clouds of dust.

Its head tilted from side to side as it lurched blindly forward. *SCRAPE . . . SCRAPE . . .*

All around me, startled cries turned to moans of horror.

"The curse!" a man yelled. "The curse of Pukrah!"

"Pukrah walks!" General Rameer choked out. He began backing up, his face twisted in shock.

The lights darted over the mummy as it leaned forward, staggering stiffly, arms outstretched. And then the circles of light swung away — and swept over the cave walls as General Rameer's men turned away.

A rush of light toward the cave entrance.

Moaning in terror, whispering their shock, the men followed the light. They stampeded over the rock-strewn floor, kicking up thick curtains of dust.

The darting lights swirled in the rising dust. Strange shadows slid toward the cave opening beside the fleeing men.

It reminded me of an old black-and-white movie, all out of focus, running at the wrong speed.

I stood as if hypnotized, watching. Watching . . .

I watched General Rameer duck his head as he shot out of the cave entrance, into an orange shaft of morning sunlight. I watched his men follow, running in panic, squeezing through the entrance, out of the cave, and still running.

I've got to run too, I suddenly realized.

The strange scene had frozen me in place. The cold horror had paralyzed me.

But now I knew I had to follow the others. I turned to run — too late.

Too late!

The mummy — Pukrah's mummy — was on me.

The ancient arms rose up in my face.

The mummy grabbed me!

Grabbed me by the throat with its ancient, dusty hands.

So strong . . . so inhumanly strong . . .

It wrapped its hands around my throat and started to squeeze.

20

"Noooo —" I choked out.

The mummy loosened its grip. The gauzed hands slid away.

Pukrah tilted back his head. And from beneath the heavy covering, I heard laughter.

I staggered back, rubbing my throat. My heart thudded in my chest. I struggled to see through the billowing curtain of dust.

"Pukrah —" I murmured.

The mummy raised its hands to its face and began clawing at the bandages.

I stared in shock as it pulled bandages loose.

"Michael — help me!" it cried, its voice muffled behind the gauze. Its hands pulled helplessly at the bandages.

"Michael — get this stuff off!"

"Huh?" I swallowed hard and stared in disbelief. "Megan?"

"Of course. Megan," she replied. "Who else? Get this off! I can't breathe!"

I took a deep breath and stepped forward to help her. I shoved her hands away and began tearing bandages from her face.

"Megan — good job!" I exclaimed. "But how —?"

"It took all morning," she groaned.

I unwrapped several layers, and her face appeared, damp from sweat. "Didn't you notice I wasn't around this morning?" she asked.

"Well . . . I looked for you," I replied. "But —"

I unwrapped her hands. Then we both began tugging the gauze off the rest of her.

"Megan — you scared me to death!" I cried. "Why didn't you tell me what you were doing?"

"How could I?" she replied. "The general had you watched night and day. I couldn't get near you."

She stepped out from the pile of bandages. She had wrapped the stuff around her clothes, around her boots.

"But — why?" I choked out.

"I was worried about you, Michael," she replied, pulling gauze from her hair. "In your tent last night, you were sweating. You seemed so totally stressed. I thought maybe you were lying to me."

"Maybe . . ." I muttered, embarrassed.

"So I checked out the cave last night," Megan continued. "And guess what? No mummy. So I knew I had to think fast. I had to think of a way to save your life — until you can find the real hiding place."

Her eyes locked on mine. "You *do* know the hiding place, don't you?"

I didn't have a chance to answer.

We both screamed as we saw the soldiers burst into the cave, rifles raised.

About a dozen black-uniformed soldiers.

Rebel soldiers.

"It's the boy!" one of them cried.

"The boy and Rameer's daughter!" another rebel exclaimed.

They blocked the cave entrance.

"Don't move," one of them said, moving toward us, his dark eyes darting from Megan to me, his rifle in front of his chest. "You will come with us."

"You — you're going to *rescue* us?" I cried.

He snickered. His eyes remained icy cold. "Not quite."

ebel vans and Jeeps had pulled up to the rock cliff. Megan and I were forced into the back of a black van. The windows had been painted over. We couldn't see out.

A grim-faced rebel soldier, lean and bearded, a black beret tilted over his forehead, kept a pistol on us from the seat in front.

The van bounced over the desert. We roared over the sand, tires spinning loudly.

Megan and I huddled unhappily in the back, our hands clasped tightly in our laps. "What are they going to do to us?" I whispered.

Megan shrugged. "They could do anything," she whispered back. Her chin trembled. "They are more evil than the general and his men. Much more evil and desperate."

That news didn't cheer me up.

After about an hour, the van squealed to a stop. The bearded soldier jumped out quickly and pulled open the back door. He motioned with his pistol for Megan and me to climb out.

We stepped out into blinding sunlight. Two rows of black canvas tents stretched in a flat, sandy clearing in front of us, hidden by tall rock cliffs.

A tall, powerful-looking man strode out of the first tent. He had long, curly black hair, black eyes under heavy black eyebrows, a scowl on his tanned face. He wore baggy black trousers and an oversized black shirt, unbuttoned, revealing a broad, tanned chest.

"Here they are, General Mohamm. The two prisoners," the soldier said, motioning to Megan and me with his pistol.

The general eyed us both without smiling. "Are you General Rameer's adopted daughter?" he asked Megan.

She nodded.

"That makes us cousins," he said, a tiny smile creasing his face. "General Rameer is my cousin."

"He says you are a traitor," Megan sneered.

The general's eyes flared angrily. He turned to me. "And you are the one they hid in America?"

"I — I guess," I stammered.

I concentrated on keeping my knees from shaking.

General Mohamm took a step closer. His expression turned menacing. "You are the son of the former leaders? You are the one with the secret of Pukrah's mummy hidden in your brain?"

"I don't know!" I cried. "My name is Michael Clarke. I grew up in Long Island, New York. I don't know anything —"

General Mohamm rubbed the black stubble on his chin. "General Rameer cannot rule without the mummy," he said thoughtfully. "If I find the mummy before he does, he will have to pay attention to me."

"But I don't know anything!" I protested.

"We are wasting time," the general said, scowling. He motioned to two black-uniformed soldiers who stood at the side of his tent. They came hurrying over.

"Take the boy to the operating tent," General Mohamm ordered. "Let's find this computer chip. Now."

22

I took off.

I couldn't let them slice open my head.

I dove past General Mohamm.

He uttered a cry. Grabbed for me. Missed.

I cut sharply. My legs nearly fell out from under me as I slid around the side of his tent. Shooting out both arms to catch my balance, I flew past a long row of tents.

"Go, Michael! Go, Michael!"

I could hear Megan cheering me on.

I reached the last tent in the row. Spun back. Then turned toward the desert.

Where to run?

Where could I go?

My eyes swept in one direction, then the other.

I knew I couldn't outrun them. And I couldn't see any place to hide in the flat sands of the clearing.

Don't stop to think, Michael! I scolded myself. Just run!

I spun away from the rebel camp and took off over the sand.

My shoes sank in the soft sand. I kept slipping. I felt as if I weighed a thousand pounds.

But I forced myself to run.

I didn't get far.

Several black-uniformed soldiers caught up to me easily.

They surrounded me, rifles raised. Their faces were blank. Their eyes cold. They didn't say a word.

I struggled to catch my breath as they hustled me back to General Mohamm at the front of the camp.

He shook his head and frowned at me. His dark eyes gazed at me, almost sadly. "There is nowhere to run, Michael," he said softly.

Megan stood between two soldiers. "At least you tried!" she called to me.

"Take him," the general ordered his men. "Watch him closely. He may be foolish enough to try again."

The soldiers grabbed my arms, but I pulled free. "Please!" I cried.

The general had already started back to his tent. He turned at the sound of my cry.

"Please don't cut open my head!" I begged.

For some reason, that made him chuckle.

He shook his head, smiling as if I'd said something funny.

"Please —" I repeated.

The soldiers grabbed me again. They pulled me roughly, nearly lifting me off the ground.

"Let him go!" I heard Megan cry angrily. "Hey — let him go!"

But of course the soldiers ignored her.

And dragged me into the surgery tent.

White-gowned doctors were waiting there.

The soldiers forced me onto my back on a high metal table.

The doctors strapped down my hands and feet. They covered me with a heavy blanket.

Then they raised a large metal machine over me and prepared to operate.

"**N**o!" I cried.

I struggled to free myself, twisting my legs, straining my arms against the straps.

No. I couldn't budge them.

The doctors lowered a section of the machine and swung it around to point at my head.

"Please —" I cried. "Don't cut my head open. Don't open my brain —"

A young doctor with wavy black hair poking out of his clear plastic surgical cap leaned over me. His dark eyes locked on mine. "We're not going to cut you," he said.

I swallowed. "Huh? You're not?"

He shook his head. "We're not going to cut you. We're going to X-ray you."

"Ohhhhhh."

A long sigh of relief escaped my mouth.

"You can relax," the doctor said, patting my chest. "It isn't going to hurt. You are very lucky. We stole this X-ray machine from a hospital across the border."

I shut my eyes. I was so happy.

They don't have to open my brain. They just have to photograph it.

But then what? I suddenly wondered, my eyes shooting open, my heart beginning to race again.

What will they do when they see there is no memory chip?

Or what if they *find* a memory chip?

What will they do then? Go in and *get* it?

The equipment buzzed and hummed. At least they told the truth about one thing — it was painless.

"We should steal a CAT-scan machine," I heard a doctor murmur.

"How are we going to power one of those out in the desert?" another doctor replied.

More buzzing and humming.

And then the machine was lifted and swung away.

"Wait here," a doctor told me.

Did I have a choice?

The doctors disappeared. The tent stood empty. I lay there, listening to voices outside the tent.

A fly landed on my cheek. I couldn't swat it off.

I shook my head hard. The fly walked up my cheek to my forehead.

I could feel its sticky legs move on my hot skin. It made my whole body tingle and itch. Sweat rolled down into my eyes.

I shook my head again. Finally, the fly darted away.

After a few minutes, I heard footsteps approaching. Voices. I expected to see the doctors. But two soldiers leaned over me.

"You're finished here," one of them said. He started to unclasp my hands and feet.

"The general wants to see you," the other soldier said.

Rubbing my sore wrists, I followed them out into the bright afternoon sunlight. My stomach growled. I realized I hadn't eaten anything all day.

As we made our way along the row of tents, I searched for Megan. But she was nowhere in sight.

The soldiers led me up to General Mohamm. He stood in front of his tent talking to a small group of men. He turned away from them when he saw me. As he came striding over to me, his dark eyes locked on mine.

"Michael," he said. "The X rays were very interesting."

"Interesting?" I choked out.

He nodded. "There's no memory chip inside

99

your brain," he said, frowning. "You're not the right boy!"

"I *knew* it!" I blurted out. "I *knew* it!"

"You're not the prince," General Mohamm sneered. "You are an imposter. We have no use for you."

"Yes!" I cried happily. "Yes! What does that mean? Does that mean that I can go home now?"

He ignored me. His frown grew deeper. The light seemed to fade from his eyes.

He turned to the two soldiers who had remained close at my sides.

"You two," he said softly, "take Michael out to the desert and kill him."

o way!" I cried.

Once again I tried to run.

And once again I was easily caught by the general's black-uniformed soldiers.

"Take him," General Mohamm repeated. He motioned with his head toward the desert. "He has wasted our time."

The soldiers started to drag me away.

But another soldier — an enormous man — came bouncing up to the general. Big and broad, built like a buffalo, he had long, curly black hair flying around his face and a black eye patch over one eye.

"Wait!" he cried breathlessly, holding up two huge hands.

"What is the problem, Raoul?" the general asked sharply.

The two soldiers continued to grip my arms tightly. But they stopped to hear what Raoul was saying.

"Is the boy an American citizen?" he asked General Mohamm.

The general rubbed his stubbled chin. "I don't know. Why does it matter?"

"We don't want trouble with the U.S.," the big man said, breathing hard from his run.

The general narrowed his dark eyes thoughtfully.

"When we defeat Rameer and take over the kingdom, we want the U.S. to be our friend," Raoul said. "So let the boy go. Do not kill him."

Yesssss! I thought. *Listen to him, General. Please — listen to him!*

"No," General Mohamm said, shaking his head. "I cannot let him go. He has seen our camp. He will tell Rameer where we are hiding."

"But the U.S. government —" Raoul started.

"They will never know." The general cut him off. "And if they find out the boy died, we will tell them it was not us. That General Rameer had him killed."

Raoul stared at the general for a long moment, still breathing hard. Finally, he shrugged his huge shoulders and tossed up his hands. "Fine, General. Have it your way. The boy must die."

"No — wait!" I cried. "There's no reason to kill

me! I — I can't give away your hiding place. I don't have any idea where we are!"

The soldiers began to drag me away.

"How are you going to kill him?" I heard Raoul ask. "You cannot shoot him, General. Our bullets can be traced to us. We don't want anyone to know that —"

"Take him to the python pit," the general commanded the soldiers. "The pythons have not been fed in a while. The boy will make a good meal."

dug my heels into the sand. I thrashed my arms and tried to pull free.

But the soldiers were too strong. They pulled me easily, past the rows of canvas tents, out over the flat yellow sand.

Python pit? *Python pit?*

The words repeated in my mind. Each time they repeated, my throat felt tighter, my legs felt heavier, my heart pounded faster.

Python pit?

They don't really have a snake pit dug into the sand — do they? I wondered.

They're not really going to feed me to pythons — are they?

I stared out at the desert. The afternoon sun made the sand sparkle like gold, so bright I had to squint.

The only sound was our breathing and the *WHUSH WHUSH* of our shoes sinking into the sand as we walked.

I glanced back and saw that General Mohamm and Raoul were following us. Their faces were grim. They stared straight ahead, avoiding my eyes.

Up ahead in the shimmering distance, I saw a black pennant waving on a tall stick. As we came closer, I saw a dark opening, a wide circle in the sand beside the pennant.

A pit. Cut deep in the sand.

We stopped at its edge. I tried to squirm away. But the silent soldiers gripped me tightly.

I tried to swallow but my throat ached from dryness.

I peered down into the pit.

And saw the pythons down below, crawling over each other, curling, twisting around each other.

"Ohhhh." A horrified moan escaped my lips.

They were so big! Could they be real? Were there really pythons as fat as fire hoses?

The snakes were tan and gray. They raised their heads from the bottom of the pit as if trying to reach me. Twisting and curling, they peered up at me with wet black eyes.

Hungry eyes.

Their mouths opened eagerly, wide mouths with long black darting tongues.

They can swallow me, I realized, trembling hard

now, trembling so hard, I leaned against the soldiers to keep from tumbling down into the pit.

They can swallow me whole.

The python heads stretched up. Banged and bumped against each other. Stretched ... stretched eagerly ...

"They are fighting for position," one of the soldiers said.

"The pythons are hungry today," General Mohamm said softly from just behind me.

"I have never seen them so eager," Raoul agreed.

The soldiers dragged me closer to the edge of the pit. The toes of my shoes hung over the side.

General Mohamm moved to my side. He stared at me coldly. "Michael, do you have anything you want to tell me now? Anything you want to say that might save your life?"

"Please —" I struggled to choke out more words, but they wouldn't come. "Please —"

"Do you have anything to say?" the general repeated.

"No. I — I —" I sputtered.

The pythons stretched their heads up, tilted them back, opened their gaping mouths.

"Wait! Stop!"

I heard a familiar voice from behind us.

"Wait!"

I turned my head and saw Megan running full-speed, waving her arms frantically.

"Wait!" she cried. "I have an idea!"

stared out the plane window at the desert far below. The plane turned slowly into the sunlight.

I shielded my eyes from the bright light. When I could look down again, I saw the sparkling blue ocean come into view.

I gripped the seat arms tightly, as if I didn't believe they were real.

Was I really in an airplane heading home?

I turned to Megan in the seat beside me. "You're a genius!" I declared, shouting over the roar of the jet engines.

She smiled. "I know," she replied.

"Another two seconds, and I'd be python meat," I said, shaking my head.

"No. That's not true," Megan said, her smile fading. She leaned close to talk, even though we were the only two passengers on the plane.

"They never planned to drop you into that pit," she insisted. "They are cruel men. But they aren't totally evil."

"I couldn't come much closer!" I cried. "My feet were over the edge. The pythons' tongues were lapping at my shoes!"

I shuddered. I could still picture those shiny, wet eyes, those gaping mouths.

"They use that pit to frighten people," Megan replied. "They don't feed people to the snakes."

"Then why —?" I started.

"They wanted to give you one more chance to tell them where the mummy is hidden," Megan explained. "They knew you didn't have the memory chip. But they thought you might know anyway. They were making one last try to scare the information out of you."

I nodded. "I get it."

I settled into the seat and stared back out the window. Nothing but blue-green ocean down there. I really was heading home!

I shut my eyes and remembered Megan's speech to General Mohamm.

"Send Michael back to the United States," she told him. "And if you really want to defeat my father, send me to the United States with Michael."

"How will that defeat your father?" General Mohamm sneered.

"Sending me away will make my father furious and out of his head with worry," Megan replied. "He will think I have been kidnapped. It will break his heart and his spirit. He will drop everything. He will even forget about this war — in order to track me down."

General Mohamm thought about it a long while. And then, finally, he ordered: "Send them both away."

I gripped the arms of the airplane seat and turned to Megan. "Your idea was totally brilliant!" I told her.

"Well . . . it worked." She grinned at me. "He actually believed that General Rameer and I are close!" She laughed.

I laughed too.

Here we were, on a big passenger jet, flying away from Jezekiah and all its dangers. Heading to JFK Airport near my home in Long Island.

"What do you plan to do when we reach New York?" I asked.

Her smile faded. She shrugged. "I — I don't really know."

"Well, you can come home with me," I told her. "Mom and Dad —"

I stopped.

Were they my mom and dad?

Would they come pick me up at the airport?

Would they be glad to see me? Could I go back to my old life?

All these frightening questions swept through my mind.

Questions without answers.

I sank down in the seat, shut my eyes, and tried not to think.

The plane landed that night. As we cruised slowly to the gate, I felt so nervous I thought I'd jump out of my skin.

Megan and I ran through the terminal.

I dodged a baggage cart. Nearly tumbled into a group of teenagers. Stumbled up to a pay phone.

I glimpsed Megan behind me. "Good luck," she said. She raised both hands. She had her fingers crossed.

I dropped a quarter into the slot and dialed my number.

My hand was shaking so hard, I could barely hold onto the phone.

One ring. Two . . .

Mom answered after the third ring.

"It's me!" I cried. "I'm *here*!"

"Who?" Mom replied. "Who *is* this?"

y heart sank.

"It's me — Michael!" I shouted over the noise of the airport, pressing the receiver tightly to my ear.

"Michael? You're back?" she cried. "I don't believe it! I never expected — I mean, I'm so *happy*!"

I let out a long sigh of relief. I turned and flashed Megan a thumbs-up.

She grinned back at me.

"Where are you?" Mom cried. "At JFK? Your dad and I will be right there!"

As soon as I arrived home, I went running around the house like a madman. I totally freaked out! I wanted to kiss the floor.

Mom kept hugging me every two seconds. Dad kept wiping tears from his eyes.

They welcomed Megan warmly. We all sat down in the living room, and I tried to tell them everything that happened to me.

Mom and Dad listened quietly as I talked. When I told them the scary parts, they shook their heads and groaned.

"Do you believe *any* of this?" I asked, finishing my long story. "And it turned out I was the wrong kid. They had the wrong kid all along!"

Mom and Dad exchanged a long glance.

Mom leaned across the couch toward me. "But, Michael," she said softly, putting a hand on my arm. "You are the *right* kid. You *are* the prince of Jezekiah!"

gasped. "No way!" I choked out.

They both nodded solemnly.

Megan stared across the room at me, clasping and unclasping her hands tensely in her lap.

"Yes," Mom and Dad replied in unison.

"We are not your real parents, Michael," Dad said, speaking slowly and just above a whisper. "Your real parents were the leaders of the kingdom."

"The story General Rameer told you is true," Mom revealed. "All of it. When war broke out in Jezekiah, we brought you here to Long Island to keep you safe."

"But that's impossible!" I protested. I jumped to my feet. "That can't be true! They X-rayed me for the memory chip. It isn't there. I don't have any memory chip planted in my brain!"

"We know," Dad replied, still speaking softly, calmly. He motioned for me to sit down.

But I stood over him, trembling.

"We had the memory chip removed when you were a baby," Mom told me. "We knew it could ruin your life."

"But — but —" I sputtered. "You sent me away last week! You sent me to Jezekiah!"

"We had no choice," Dad said. "We had to send you when General Rameer called for you."

"But we prayed you would be sent home when it was discovered you didn't have the chip," Mom added. She sighed happily. "And you were!"

She mopped at her eyes with a tissue. "It worked. They sent you home, safe and sound."

Dad stood up and hugged me. Then he took my arm and started to lead me out of the living room. He motioned for Mom and Megan to follow.

"Dad — what's up?" I demanded. "Where are we going?"

"I know you've had many surprises, Michael," he replied, his expression solemn. "But I have one more for you."

29

Dad clicked on the light to the basement.

The four of us trooped down the creaking wooden stairs.

A tall antique wardrobe stood against the back wall. It had been there since I was tiny.

"Help me with this," Dad asked.

The two of us pushed hard and slid the heavy wardrobe to the side. I stepped back, wiping my hands on my jeans — and saw a narrow wooden door cut into the basement wall.

"Huh?"

Dad unbolted the hidden door and pulled it open.

He clicked on another light. We peered inside a tiny square closet.

Megan and I both cried out when we saw the

dark wood mummy case tilted up against the stone wall.

With a groan, Dad lifted the heavy lid.

And we stared at Pukrah.

Stared at the ancient mummy that two armies had fought over for twelve years.

"It — it's here!" I finally choked out.

Mom nodded. "The best hiding place we could think of," she said. "We smuggled it out with us when we took you to live in America. We've kept the mummy and the sapphire safe and sound all these years."

"Wow," Megan murmured, stepping up to the case, staring wide-eyed at the ancient, gauzed figure. "Wow."

I was so totally wired. I thought I would never get to sleep that night.

But I was so happy to be back in my own bed, I fell asleep as soon as my head sank into the pillow. I slept a deep, dreamless sleep.

When I awoke, bright sunlight was already streaming in through my bedroom window.

"I'm home!" I cried joyfully, sitting up and stretching. "I'm home to stay!"

I got dressed quickly. And hurried down the hall to the room my parents had given Megan. "Hey — Megan!" I called in. "Megan?"

No answer.

I knocked on the door. "Are you up?"

No answer.

Did she wake up early and go down to breakfast? How late *was* it?

I pushed open her door and peeked inside. The bed was made. I didn't see any of her clothes.

"Huh?" I spotted a white envelope taped to the dresser mirror.

A note?

Yes. I crossed the room, tore the envelope off the mirror, and pulled out a short note. My eyes bulged in disbelief as I read the neatly handwritten words:

Michael,

I hope you will not think that I'm a bad person. I enjoyed our adventures together. And I enjoyed getting to know you.

I'm afraid I told you one little lie.

You see, my new father, General Rameer, and I really are very close. We love each other. And I would do anything to help him.

I have to confess: I didn't sneak into your room at the palace. He sent me to spy on you. This is why I was allowed to travel everywhere you went.

When I pretended to be Pukrah's mummy in the cave, I did it to make you trust me. We knew you were the right boy. I thought if you trusted me, you'd tell me the truth. We would try *anything* to find out where Pukrah was hidden.

117

And so I've been working for my father the whole time.

I'm so sorry I had to lie. You're a great guy. I hope you will understand.

Your friend,
Megan

I read the note three times, my head spinning. Then, clenching it tightly in my fist, I went running down the stairs.

"Mom! Dad! You'd better check this out!"

I found them both in the kitchen. They both looked up from the table. "Michael? What's wrong?"

"Have you seen Megan this morning?" I asked breathlessly.

"No. I thought she was still asleep."

"You'd better read this!" I cried. "I found it in her room." I shoved the note in front of them.

They read it quickly, their eyes wide, mouths dropping open.

"Uh-oh," Dad murmured.

That's all he said. Then he jumped up and ran to the basement stairs.

Mom and I were close behind him. We flew down the stairs.

Dad didn't have to turn on the light. We could see that the door to the hidden basement room was wide open.

The mummy case was open too.

The case stood empty.

Empty except for another note on the bottom.

I grabbed up the note. I recognized Megan's handwriting.

"What does it say?" Dad asked in a whisper.

I read it out loud:

"THE MUMMY WALKS AGAIN."

About R.L. Stine

R.L. Stine is the most popular author in America. He is the creator of the *Goosebumps, Give Yourself Goosebumps, Fear Street,* and *Ghosts of Fear Street* series, among other popular books. He has written over 250 scary novels for kids. Bob lives in New York City with his wife, Jane, teenage son, Matt, and dog, Nadine.